A NOTE TO PARENTS

Reading Aloud with Your Child

Research shows that reading books aloud is the single most valuable support parents can provide in helping children learn to read.

- Be a ham! The more enthusiasm you display, the more your child will enjoy the book.
- Run your finger underneath the words as you read to signal that the print carries the story.
- Leave time for examining the illustrations more closely; encourage your child to find things in the pictures.
- Invite your youngster to join in whenever there's a repeated phrase in the text.
- Link up events in the book with similar events in your child's life.
- If your child asks a question, stop and answer it. The book can be a means to learning more about your child's thoughts.

Listening to Your Child Read Aloud

The support of your attention and praise is absolutely crucial to your child's continuing efforts to learn to read.

- If your child is learning to read and asks for a word, give it immediately so that the meaning of the story is not interrupted. DO NOT ask your child to sound out the word.
- On the other hand, if your child initiates the act of sounding out, don't intervene.
- If your child is reading along and makes what is called a miscue, listen for the sense of the miscue. If the word "road" is substituted for the word "street," for instance, no meaning is lost. Don't stop the reading for a correction.
- If the miscue makes no sense (for example, "horse" for "house"), ask your child to reread the sentence because you're not sure you understand what's just been read.
- Above all else, enjoy your child's growing command of print and make sure you give lots of praise. *You are your child's first teacher—and the most important one. Praise from you is critical for further risk-taking and learning.*

—Priscilla Lynch
Ph.D., New York University
Educational Consultant

For Santa's friends
all around the world
— L.K.

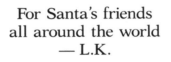

Copyright © 1994, 1981 by Leonard Kessler.
All rights reserved. Published by Scholastic Inc.
HELLO READER! and CARTWHEEL BOOKS are registered trademarks
of Scholastic Inc.

Library of Congress Cataloging-in-Publication Data

Kessler, Leonard P., 1920-
That's not Santa! / by Leonard Kessler.
p.   cm. — (Hello reader! Level 1)
Summary: When Santa cannot find his red suit, he tries on a cowboy
suit, a baseball uniform, and other clothes, but none seems right
for his yearly rounds.
ISBN 0-590-48140-1
1. Santa Claus—Juvenile fiction. [1. Santa Claus—Fiction.
2. Christmas—Fiction.] I. Title. II. Series.
PZ7.K484Th   1994
[E]—dc20   93-39653   CIP   AC

12 11 10 9 8 7 6 5   5 6 7 8 9/9

Printed in the U.S.A.   **24**

First Scholastic printing, October 1994

THAT'S NOT SANTA!

Story and pictures
by Leonard Kessler

Hello Reader! — Level 1

SCHOLASTIC INC.
Cartwheel B·O·O·K·S®

New York   Toronto   London   Auckland   Sydney

December 24 . . .

It is the day before Christmas.
Santa's sleigh is filled
with toys.
Everything is ready
for Santa's trip.

But where is Santa?

Santa is sleeping.

"Time to get up.
Time to put on my red suit,"
he says.

Santa looks for his red suit.

He looks everywhere.

"Have you seen my red suit?"

"Have you seen my red suit?"
No one has seen Santa's
red suit.

"No red suit.
No Christmas!"

"NO CHRISTMAS?"

"Wait. I have an idea."

Santa goes upstairs.

"How's this?"

"Oh, no. You can't go out
like that.
That's not Santa!"

"Wait. Wait.
I'll be right back,"
Santa says.

"How about this?"

"Or this?"

"This okay?"

"What do you think?"

"No, no, no.
That's not Santa!"

"Wait. I'll be right back."

"This is it!
Off I go."

"No, no, no.
You can't go out
in your underwear.
That's not Santa!"

Mrs. Claus comes home.
"You can't go out that way.
You will catch a cold."

"But he can't find his
red suit."

"Red suit?
Santa, I want you to open
your Christmas present
right now."

"A new red suit!
I'll put it right on.
Thank you."

"NOW THAT'S SANTA!"

"It's getting late.
We have to go."

"We?"

"Ho, ho, ho.
I'm going with you.
I have a red suit, too."

"Ho, ho, ho.
This Christmas will be
twice as much fun!"